GRACE

Rescuing Robert

By Jenny O'Brien

Copyright © 2017 by Jenny O'Brien

All rights reserved. This book or any portion thereof may not be reproduced or used in any manner whatsoever without the express written permission of the publisher except for the use of brief quotations in a book review

This book is a work of fiction. Any resemblance to actual persons, living or dead is entirely co-incidental.

The moral right of the author has been asserted
All Rights reserved

Also by Jenny O'Brien

Ideal Girl
Girl Descending
Unhappy Ever After Girl

Englishman in Blackpool (short story)
Englishwoman in Paris
Englishwoman in Manhattan
Englishwoman in Scotland

For children
Boy Brainy

Praise for Jenny O'Brien

"I absolutely adored this story. It was fun, flirty, romantic, tragic, emotionally heart-breaking at times but also very heart-warming." Kraftireader book blog.

"This author has a true gift. All her books are easy reading with a story to tell that keeps you wondering what next." Booklover Bev

"Another wonderful, romantic cosy read beautifully written with warmth love and tenderness." Michele Turner.

"Really romantic and quite sexy. Went straight on to her next book which I am just starting - an Englishwoman in Manhattan." Dawn McCaulay

Dedicated to Michele Turner

'If you are going through hell – keep going…'
   Sir Winston Churchill

Chapter One
4th June, 1940 Rose Cottage, Ramsgate

"The Admiralty want men experienced in marine internal combustion engines or services in yachts or motorboats".

"Nowhere in that sentence is the word girl mentioned."
"But grandfather…"
"No buts. To allow a twenty year old girl cross the English Channel by herself is not happening on my watch."

She glared at him. "If you think I'm going to sit around waiting for someone else to rescue Robert then you've got another thing coming. We've stood waiting at the harbour now for five days, five whole days and nothing. No sign. No news. Nothing. He's my brother and, apart from you the only living relative I have."
She knelt by his feet, both hands now on his knees as she peered up at him through a cloud of hair. "I have to

do something, pop. I love you, I really do. The way you took us in last year after… Well, I can't lose him too, I just can't."

"Even if I let you have the keys it's not up to me. They won't let you go. Nowhere in that announcement did they say girls…"

"Well, I'll tuck my hair under a hat. With oilskins and wellies they'll never suspect."

*

It was chaos, unorganised chaos on this the last day of *Operation Dynamo*, the civilian-led evacuation of Dunkirk. With boats gathering at Ramsgate from as far as The Isle of Man and Scotland everyone and anyone with anything even half-seaworthy queued up to follow the steady stream of boats out the mouth of the harbour.

The sea was calm; the only light coming from the bright stars and the little lanterns swinging on the masts of the smaller sailboats. There was nothing to see apart from the shadows and shapes of the other vessels, nothing at all until the early red mist of dawn. But Sally, last in a long line, knew it couldn't be the dawn, not at 3 am. It was the sight of Dunkirk burning that blazed its fiery glow across the waters. And then there was the droning sound of aircraft overhead as German bombers continued to wreak havoc on the already decimated town. Manoeuvring the barge even closer, she saw the line of men shoulder deep in the waves patiently waiting to be ferried to the heaving trawlers and ships that couldn't reach the beach; patiently waiting while being showered with bullets.

 Pulling her hat further down she scanned the shore and the scattered remains of fallen men interspersed with ambulances and jeeps, their doors open; empty and abandoned. How could she find him, one man in thousands, hundreds of thousands; their shadows merging to one congealed blob of black?

 She reached the first men, the waters straining up to their necks. Her eyes settled on the one nearest; a man, a tall man with the biggest smile imaginable.

"Of all the boats I never expected to see an itty bitty houseboat," his hand running over the bright pink hull. "Are you sure it's seaworthy?"

"You'd better hope it is." She leaned over the side, her hand grasping his arm as she helped him over the gunnel.

"Why, it's only a gi…"

"Shush for Heaven's sake. I'm here to help so what does it matter?"

"What indeed," his gaze fixed on the clear blue of her eyes.

"I'm looking for someone. A man."

His eyebrow arched even as his smile broadened. "It's your lucky day, then. Men we aren't short of," his arm now stretched out to help another soldier clamber over the side. "If we load the inside first," he added, but not to her, to the man now standing on his left. "Pack them in tight as you can, Jim."

"My brother."

"What? Jim's your brother?" She had his attention now, although she didn't like his response.

"Not Jim. The man I'm looking for."

"And just how the hell do you think we're going to be able to find one man amongst all this lot?" he asked, scanning the sea now heaving with troops, even as he dropped his hand to help the next man board.

"I don't know," her voice breaking. "All I know is I must try. Robert's all I have now. He's injured…"

"Injured?"

"Leg, broken leg. He's also my twin if that helps?"

"Your twin, but does he look like you?" His eyes scrunched up as he tried to look at her face, or what little there was to see.

"Same hair." She laughed and suddenly it was as if half the beach turned in their direction but she didn't care. This was the only chance she'd have so, ripping off her hat, she allowed her thick curly black hair tumble around her face before bending her head and packing it back out of sight.

He turned, clapping the man beside him on the back. "Ian, you continue loading. Take as many as you can, about twenty I'm guessing and look after…' He paused, his eyes seeking hers.

"Sally."

"Look after Sally. If I'm not back in ten minutes go without me."

"Sir?"

But he'd stopped listening. Throwing her one last look he stepped onto the side of the gunnel before diving into the swelling sea.

"Right then miss, you stay over there by the wheel out the way and I'll sort this out."

"How did you know I was a…?"

"A girl? Begging your pardon, miss, but it stands out a mile. Best you keep out the way. It's a long time since these men have seen anything like you," he added, his eyes on her coal black hair starting to come adrift from under her cap. "The captain will be back in a minute, you just wait and see. He always comes through."

*

Damn bloody stupid woman. What the hell does she think she's doing coming all this way, and by herself too?

He ran in the wrong direction up the beach, as he continued muttering to himself at the stupidity of the female race. She was lucky it had been him and Ian. She'd be safe with Ian. And he only hoped she'd be safe with him as he felt something shift in his groin at the memory of those innocent, pink, rosebud lips demanding to be kissed. He tried to tell himself she was only a young chit of a girl, probably only just out of the schoolroom but his groin wasn't interested in common sense. That part of his body had suddenly gone deaf to all thoughts except for one while his brain struggled on trying to remember just where he'd seen that hair.

It had been on a boy scarcely old enough to be out of long trousers, which would figure if he was her twin.

He'd been lying on a stretcher by one of the abandoned ambulances presumably waiting for someone to come back for him. He'd even tried to help only to be shouted away. But now he was back and he wouldn't take no for an answer, his eyes searching until he found what he was looking for.

Trying to manhandle a grumpy, bad-tempered - not to mention - injured man down the beach, a man that matched him in breadth and probably height was going to take all his strength and ingenuity. It was also lunacy, his lunacy to help a man on crutches across an open beach in sight of the aeroplanes. But one look into her pleading eyes he had no choice, even if he died in the attempt.

"Well, well, well, it's Sally's little brother as I live and breathe. Fancy meeting you here, although I must say, I was more surprised at the sight of your sister. Not a place for a lady, unless she isn't, that is?" His eyebrows arched.

"What?"

At least he'd managed to get his attention, which was more than he'd managed before. "Your sister, I was asking if she was...?"

"I know what you were asking. I know what you were insinuating and I'll have your life for implying my sister's virtue is in any way compromised," he screamed, reaching for his crutches and trying to heave himself to standing, beads of sweat collecting on his brow.

"Good."

"Good?" He paused, as he tried to gain his balance on the sand with his one good leg, the other stretched out before him.

"Yes, good, and I'm sure you'd like to ensure it remains that way," he added, glancing around at the rows upon rows of cowered but never defeated soldiers. "These are gentlemen to a man but she is the only woman on the beach or at least I hope she is."

"Sally's here?"

"Yes, although if she has any sense she'll take that houseboat of hers, frilly floral curtains and all, and be gone from this hellhole. This isn't any place for the likes of her. It isn't any place for the likes of us either for that matter," he added, almost to himself, his eyes now on the skyline and the number of Messerschmitts hovering overhead. "Here, let me help you," he said, taking his arm and not accepting no for an answer.

*

    The trip back was slow, so slow. They were hardly moving but with the cabin stuffed to the brim with soldiers, they were lucky to be moving at all. Captain William Darty of the East Lancashire Regiment only stopped boarding when the tough little houseboat threatened to sink under the weight of its heavy load. By the time they'd reached the safety of Ramsgate harbour and the hero's welcome that awaited, the boat was scarcely afloat but that didn't matter. Nothing mattered except the safety of the men on board.

    Sally tried to keep out of the way with one arm around Robert, his face drenched in sweat; his brow wrinkled with pain. She allowed the men to hug her briefly, all her energies now on how to get him home.

"Here, let me."

She found herself standing on her own as William scooped up Robert, all thirteen stone of him, and started up the slipway. "If you can grab the crutches and lead the way. I'm good for about 200 yards…" he added over his shoulder. But he needn't have worried. One of the many cars at the top took pity on them and within minutes they found themselves outside a little, two-bedroomed cottage hidden under a screen of trailing pink roses.

"I think it's exhaustion as much as anything. Give him a few hours and get the doctor if you're worried." They were standing looking down at Robert as he lay stretched across the candlewick bedspread, his black hair moist against his forehead. "If you would like me to help him into bed I'm happy to?"

"We've asked enough. There's no way my grandfather and I can ever repay you…" she started, tears now hovering on the end of her lashes before tipping over to run down her cheeks.

"Well, a cuppa and a sandwich wouldn't go amiss," his brown eyes twinkling across the room.

"I can do better than that. Grandfather doesn't get up for breakfast but come down when you're ready." She met his gaze with a shy smile before leaving the room and heading into her bedroom next door.

She was well aware of how she looked, still decked out in fisherman's garb. She was well aware of how she must look to him, and she didn't want to look that way anymore. Opening her wardrobe she pulled out the only dress she owned; plain blue cotton the colour of her eyes. Her hair was another matter entirely as she peered into the mirror on her dressing table. *Bird's nest* came to mind so she just left it trailing down her back to sort out later. It was now time to cook up a feast for this tall quiet stranger who'd helped save Robert.

They had lots of eggs and still half a loaf from yesterday. She had been saving the bangers for tonight's tea but now she tipped them out into the pan and soon the room was full of the smell of sizzling sausages. Half turning at the sound of footsteps on the old worn lino she tilted her head to the back door. "The toilet's out back if you…"

"No, I'm good. I'll just wash my hands if I may?" he added, joining her by the sink and then watching her every move.

"Is there anything I can do to help," his eyes on her face framed in a cloud of hair.

"No, I'm good."

"Good and lovely," he said joining her by the cooker; his hands now on her shoulders before reaching up to feel her hair. "I've been longing to do that ever since I…" his sentence trailed off into an unfinished jumble of half formed words before smoothing the inky black strands between his fingers.

"It's all tangled."

"It's perfect, perfect hair for the perfect girl," his eyes now on her face as his palm moved from her hair to her cheek. "Such a brave, perfect girl," he added, his lips lowering to hers.

She'd never been kissed before. No, that wasn't quite true, as she remembered all those hours practising in her room with only her mirror for company. Alice, her best friend in the whole world, had told her all about real kissing and about how, as soon as a man's lips joined yours, your body turned to putty. She'd laughed. All the innocent girls at the convent had laughed. She wasn't laughing now. In fact she was having trouble standing on legs that felt very much like… well like putty.

"The sausages," she finally managed, ripping her mouth from his.

"Ah yes, the sausages," he murmured, reaching round her back and fiddling with the switch. "The sausages are safe. You however…"

He pulled away, his face raw with emotion and something else, something she couldn't name. Confusion? Restraint? Disappointment?

"You however are safe too," he finally said, running his hand through his hair. "I'm sorry. I owe you an apology. Here you are having invited me into your house and here I am trying to..."

"To what," she repeated, her eyes wide.

Nothing in her five years at the convent had taught her about men stopping what they'd started. Alice had been most emphatic on that point. Once they'd started, once you'd felt that bulge digging into your flesh, there was no going back. She'd quite clearly felt something long and stiff prod her belly so Alice had at least been right about that part.

But him pulling away? Either Alice had lied - or he didn't fancy her enough. She was heartily sick of it. Everyone at the convent had had boyfriends, everyone except her. The mirror told her each morning that she was at least passable with clear skin and eyes the colour of the sky on a clear day. But, even Doris down the road with her funny nose and more spots than a yard of polkadot had a boyfriend, so why not her?

But, unlike both Alice and Doris, she had a debt to pay and he wasn't going to stop her from paying it. She gulped, flexing her fingers even as she focused her eyes on her target with dilated pupils.

Putting her arms around his retreating back she heaved a sigh even as she pulled him fast against her breasts before running her fingers downwards to his trousers.

"Sally, stop. You can't…?"

"Shush," she whispered, concentrating on undoing his belt, ignoring his hands clamped around her wrists, hands that decidedly slackened when she finally fiddled through the coarse fabric to find what she was looking for – the buttons to his fly.

She felt him shudder as her fingers brushed over his… She blushed. She couldn't even come up with a word for it let alone say it. But she was on a mission. After all, she was sick to death of the likes of Alice with her happy marriage and baby bump. She wanted that. She wanted that now and he wasn't going to stop her from having it.

    She moved in front of him because, instinctively she knew, with his trousers around his ankles he might find it difficult if not embarrassing to move himself. Her hand was still where she knew it shouldn't be but by the intent look on his face he didn't seem to mind. The next bit was going to be difficult, her eyes fascinated by his large appendage now it was free from his underwear. Licking her lips came automatically as she knelt on the floor in front of him, her hand reaching through his legs and cupping him just like Alice had told her. Closing her eyes, she positioned her mouth even as she grabbed his shaft in a vice-like grip.

    In truth, she was hanging on for dear life, scared he'd hate what she was doing to him. That is until she felt a tremor run the length of his body. She had him now, just like Alice had said. She had him where she wanted him, her lips and then her mouth squeezing tight. Alice said it was best to just shut your eyes and pretend it was covered in treacle. She'd never liked treacle but she did have a thing for ham...

He moved then, his hands in her hair, his head thrown back. She felt his strength; his power as he placed both hands on her head and, easing her back knelt down on the floor to join her, his lips seeking hers.

She was proud of herself, so proud. She'd repaid her debt in the only way she knew how. But now his hands moved onto her chest skimming over her breasts with a familiarity which drew a sigh from her lips. Before she knew it, he'd weaved his magic on her buttons and her dress fell open revealing her plain cotton slip, her plain, almost see-through cotton slip. She hadn't bothered with a brassiere, something he noticed straight away as his lips marked her through the fabric even as his hands reached down and dragged the slip over her head. She was naked, completely naked as the day she'd been born apart from her hand-sewn, French knickers she'd fashioned after seeing a photograph of Rita Hayworth, but they were no barrier.

His head lowered, his lips ravishing her breast as his fingers blazed a trail under the silk fabric and up to her core. Her hand fluttered to his wrist as his fingers reached their final destination but it was her turn to be shushed, his lips pressing against hers before returning to her breast where his tongue went on an intrepid expedition all of its own. "It's alright, my darling, I'm not going to hurt you…"

But she didn't hear him, all her senses in freefall as his fingers probed deep inside setting up a chain reaction of emotion she was powerless to resist.

They lay there entwined, each spent in their own way. They lay there happy and content even as he tried to pull her dress back in place.

"You're beautiful, Sally," he said into her hair, brushing a kiss across her forehead.

She laughed, her eyes on his chest and where she must have unbuttoned his shirt to get to his skin. "So are you," she replied, standing to her feet and pulling him up beside her before heading back to the cold sausages. But she needn't have worried. Sitting opposite her, he ate everything on his plate and most of everything on her plate before finally placing his knife and fork tidily in the centre.

"Sally, that was wonderful, if only every breakfast could be as good," he added with a wink.

"I think that might be quite difficult in the army."

She walked across the room, determined to finish what he'd started with that kiss. She hadn't bothered to do all the buttons on her dress and now, slipping her arms out of the sleeves, let it fall behind her in a pool of blue before stepping out of her pants. She had a blush on her face but also a smile as she shifted the table before sitting on his lap, her hair trailing across her breasts.

"Sally I can't… Sally you may…?"

"May what? Fall in love with you? Get pregnant? This is wartime, William. We have today. We have now and tomorrow?" her voice holding a question.

"Tomorrow I'll be posted, probably overseas again."

"There, you see?"

Her fingers, now familiar and increasingly brave ripped through his buttons until her bare thighs clamped around his. "Make love to me, William. Make love as if there's no war, no tomorrow. Only today," she said, reaching between his legs even as his hand covered hers, his eyes searching her face.

"If we do this, there's no going back, Sally. I'm not going to be able to stop once I've started."

"I've heard that," her hands, both of them trying to prise his fingers away.

'You've heard that," his voice incredulous. "Just who have you been speaking to?"

"Just Alice, she's very knowledgeable."

"Knowledgeable is she? Let's find out just how knowledgeable she is."

Lifting her up in the air as if she was made of glass, he gently repositioned her over his tip before lowering her on top, his arms steel around her back as she started to whimper. "It's alright, my love. The pain is only for a second…" His eyes squeezed tight from the effort of keeping it slow and easy instead of doing what instinct dictated and plunge right up to her soul and beyond…

Epilogue

4th June, 1990, Rose Cottage, Ramsgate

"Gran, Gran…wake up. You were telling me how you and Gramps rescued Great Uncle Robert," the little hand within hers starting to pull away.

"I wasn't asleep, my darling."

"Well Gramps is. I'm going to wake him up."

Sally glanced across at her husband of fifty years, her heart filling her chest even after all this time. William, the only man she'd given herself to. The only man she'd ever loved. William, who'd married her on that second morning, her grandfather and her beloved Robert the only witnesses. He'd given her three beautiful children and fifty years of happiness.

"No, leave him, pet, he's tired. Come and help me make tea while we wait for your parents. I've got your favourite sausages."

"Did someone say sausages?"

She walked across the room to where he sat stretched out in his favourite chair, a warm plaid rug across his knees. "You old fraud. We thought you were asleep?"

"Asleep," his voice indignant. "How is a man meant to sleep with you wittering on about the war?"

"Wittering? I'll give you wittering." But her voice was soft, her lips softer as she bent over him and placed a kiss against his mouth.

"I've always loved your hair," his hand reaching up and grabbing onto a curl before winding it around his finger.

"Hair is it? Hair as white as the snow we didn't get at Christmas."

"Ah, but I don't see the snow, my love. I see a girl in a blue dress with fire in her eyes and love in her heart…"

***

"Granny and Pop's are being all slushy again," her legs dangling from the chair as she took a sip of her milk.

"They're allowed to be whatever they like at their age," Alice said with a smile as she walked over to the door and pulled it closed with a smart snap. "What about a few beans to go with those sausages?"

Dear Reader

Thank you for purchasing 'Dunkirk, Rescuing Robert, all the profits of which are going to the Guernsey Branch of the British Red Cross. There is a full length follow-up planned, but that's for the future,

I have added 'Englishman in Blackpool,' the short story introduction to the Englishwoman series as an extra.

Finally thanks as always must go to my editor, Natalie Orme, for helping me whip my manuscript into shape. It is edited to UK English.

If you'd like to get in touch I'm scribblerjb on Twitter. I also have a writer page over on Facebook called Jenny O'Brien Writes, in addition I blog at Jenny O'Brien writer, over on WordPress.

Best wishes
Jenny

ENGLISHMAN IN BLACKPOOL
1997

'We only have one room left at the back. It doesn't have a sea view but I don't suppose you'll mind. I wouldn't even have that except for a cancellation this morning. This really isn't the time to be coming to Blackpool on spec you know.'

'The back room is fine Mrs...'

'Hall. But you can call me Susan, everybody does. It does have twin beds but I won't be charging you for the other one. Single gentleman, are you?'

He smiled to himself at the question: a question he'd been asked many times over the years but it still never ceased to amuse him. He'd be the last to admit he was good looking. He was nudging forty, after all and with his hair starting to show the first tentative signs of grey at the temple, he thought himself distinguished if anything. It appeared women hadn't noticed the grey or, if they had, it hadn't stopped them.

It wasn't that he didn't like women. He did. In fact, he liked all women. But it just so happened that over the years, he'd never managed to find that one special woman. He'd never stopped looking but she was as elusive as a cloud on a summer's day.

But, just because he was still a bachelor didn't mean he wanted to be bothered with stray females, not that Mrs Hall could in anyway be deserving of such a title as his eyes scrolled over her neat bobbed hair and sparkling blue eyes, but you could never tell. There was that incident a few months ago when his lordship had discovered a telephone number and a naughty message tucked into the inside pocket of his cashmere topcoat after he'd picked it up from the dry cleaners. He'd glared at him until he spotted it had been addressed to Jeeves, something he'd found incredibly funny for some unknown reason.

He suddenly realised he had yet to answer her: 'Oh, it might come in useful as my wife has been delayed, but she plans to join me later.'

She gave him a sharp glance but, instead of commenting just pushed the red book towards him before handing him a matching red plastic biro. 'Would you like the full English in the morning?'

'A full English will be fine, Susan. I'll just take my bags up to my room.'

'You do that. No lift I'm afraid. The stairs are around the corner. Enjoy your evening, Mr Hopper. My husband locks the door at midnight.'

That's good to know, in more ways than one, as he heaved a sigh at the sweetest word of all – husband!

Finally escaping, he made his way up the stairs, all the time wondering what had made him travel all the way to Blackpool. He could have booked a cheap package holiday on Costa Brava and yet here he was; in a part of the UK he didn't know and all because some woman he hadn't met in years had asked him to help her train the contestants for the next dance festival at The Winter Gardens.

He was a sucker for a sob story, he thought, plonking his bag on the spare bed before giving his surroundings a cursory glance. It didn't really matter that the carpet was 1960's swirly red and brown or that the en-suite was a fine shade of puce pink. It was clean and tidy and that's all that mattered. Propping the lid open, he removed the neatly folded shirts and trousers before shaking out his tails. He didn't really know what had possessed him to include his dress suit as his dancing days were well and truly over but, as butler to one of the most distinguished families, he was well versed in preparing for any eventuality.

'Too slow, too slow Margo and Malcolm. Too quick, Penelope and Paddy. Beverley, just perfect. Everyone just look at Beverley and her head position. Joshua, your hand…'

'My hand, Miss Peel?'

'Yes, your hand. In the Ballroom Tango, as you very well know, the man's fingers stay on his partner's back.' Her gaze fixed on his hand until he slid it back up to where it belonged.

He'd decided to walk off his double egg, sausage and bacon breakfast with a stroll down the promenade before pulling out a scrap of paper from his pocket and following the directions to the Rosebush Dance Studio, not that there were any roses in sight, but dance studios were the same the world over. It wasn't what they looked like on the outside it was the hard work, dedication and discipline on the inside that ensured the tiny studio tucked behind the bus depot was world renowned for the excellent, record-beating dancers it produced. He'd never doubted that Lavender Peel, his former dancing partner, would be successful but this successful…?

His gaze shifted from the pretty brunette, partnering Joshua *of the wandering hands* and back to his friend. He just wondered at her wisdom in asking him to help. He knew it was an emergency, what with Guy falling down the stairs, but it had been a long time, a very long time. Dancing wasn't like riding a bike and, by the amount of dust he'd had to remove from his shoes, it had been longer than he cared to admit since he'd swirled anyone around the floor. His eyes, like magnets, were drawn again to Joshua's partner as she continued to struggle with the position of his hand. A real creep if ever there was one, was his final thought before finding himself being launched at by the five foot dynamo that was Lavender Peel.

'Hopper, it's been so long.' She jumped into his arms, wrapping her wiry legs around his waist with a laugh before planting a deep kiss against his lips.

She'd always been flamboyant, or maybe he was getting staid in his old age but, gently easing her back to the ground, he felt a blush score his cheeks, his eyes careful to avoid the gaze of the performers that had stopped to watch, specifically one pair of eyes. It was as if he'd suddenly developed a location beacon in the back of his head. He gave himself a little shake: it was all very peculiar but wherever he looked all he could see was thick chestnut brown hair, yards of it coiled into a neat bun at the nape of her neck.

'Come and meet the team,' Lavender said, interrupting his thoughts with a tug on his arm. 'It's really the Ballroom Tango I'll be needing you for, the rest is all taken care of,' she added, clapping her hands to draw the attention of the dancers.

'People, this is Mr Hopper, some of you may have heard of him?' She smiled at the sight of a few nodding heads. 'That's right; the very same Mr Hopper that took the Royal Albert Hall by storm. You've seen the viral YouTube video, now here he is in person to help us rock at the Winter Gardens.' She paused, her attention now on the twelve couples standing apart, all that is except for Joshua who continued to glue himself to his partner's side.

Hopper frowned but said nothing. There was an unwritten etiquette in a dance studio and, at the moment Lavender had the floor. 'We have two days to get our act together, or rather for Hopper to see what you're made of. At the end of it we'll meet up and decide which of you are good enough to enter. Your Waltz, Quickstep, Slow Foxtrot and even your Viennese Waltz are all fantastic. I just don't know what it is about the poor little Tango that's causing all the problems…' She clapped her hands again. 'Right, back to basics and footsteps.' She turned to him. 'We break for lunch at noon for an hour. They're all yours.'

There'll all mine – Great, his eyes and his attention studiously avoiding one specific part of the room.

'Right then, as you know my name is Hopper…' He paused at the sound of a laugh from the back. Wandering through the group that parted in front of him like Moses and the Red Sea he soon found himself standing in front of Joshua.

'Well, you must admit it's funny?'

'What exactly do you find funny?'

'You a dancer, with a name like Hopper,' he said, casting his smirk around the room.

'Really? And you are called?'

'Me, I'm called?'

'Your name, or is that such a difficult concept, *Mr Me I'm Called*? After all, you do seem to have difficulty with other parts of your anatomy.' His eyes on Joshua's hands.

'Now hold on a minute…'

'No, you hold on a minute. We're here to dance. No, we're here to win. This isn't the Pleasure Beach. This isn't Blackpool Tower or the chance to appear on the telly. This is serious stuff. I suggest you start acting like an adult or you leave. The door is over there.' He swivelled on his heel, his eyes scanning the room. 'And that goes for the rest of you. You stay here and work, you work until your blisters have blisters and you have no tears left, or you go.' He stormed to the chair in the corner before sitting down and crossing his legs.

He didn't look at them. He couldn't, even if he'd wanted to. In truth, he wanted to run out of the room and head back to the safety and security of Cosgrave Manor. He'd given up dancing, a career he'd loved because he couldn't cope with dealing with prats like this Joshua chap. He wasn't made that way. All he wanted was to be left alone with a cuppa and a book and yet, here he was acting the strong alpha male, the role he despised above all others. He wasn't an alpha. He wasn't sure if he was a beta, but he wasn't a dweeb and he certainly wasn't a mug.

He could hear them shuffling from one foot to the other and loud whispers of *'Joshua, you idiot',* but he ignored them until his sixth sense kicked in for the second time in his life and he looked up into the prettiest pair of blue eyes he'd ever seen. It was the girl with the brown hair standing in front of him with a shy smile. He liked it when she smiled, his lips twitching in return.

'Yes?'

'You don't need to mind Joshua, Mr Hopper…'

'Hopper is fine. And you are?'

'Beverley. Beverley Markey. Joshua is my… my partner.'

Of course he is, his heart squeezing tight at the thought of this lovely shy girl and that odious man. Tilting his head for her to take her place back on the floor he clapped his hands.

'Right, that's the fun over. Men on the left side of the room, women on the right. This morning it's back to foot basics. This afternoon we will work on your hands.'

It was a long day, a very long day. He'd forgotten just how tiring it was and he hadn't been doing any dancing, just a lot of shouting and pulling his hair out – it was lucky he had any left. At this rate he'd be bald by the time he went home. Great two week holiday this was turning out to be although, with the competition finishing on Tuesday, he'd still have a few days to perhaps find a lake somewhere to sit beside with his rod.

He dismissed them at six and headed for the showers, keen to get changed back into his jeans and shirt. Leotards and leggings were alright but he couldn't help feeling he was reaching the age where he should stick to jogging bottoms and t-shirts as he rolled back the cuffs on his blue cotton shirt and slipped on his brown loafers. He was a free agent until the morning so he decided on a quick walk before heading to the newsagents for a couple of papers. He'd squirrel himself away in a pub with a pint or two before it was time to hunt down something to eat in one of the many cafes and restaurants that straddled the sea front.

Apart from a few hardy individuals the beach was empty. He took his time wandering to the shoreline to feel the cool water against his toes. He should have thought to bring his trunks. A nice cool swim after being stuck in a stuffy dance studio would have been just the thing to work up an appetite but, now with all the shops closed, there'd be little chance of that and commando wasn't regulation wear according to any butler's guide he'd ever come across.

    Heading back up the beach he sat down in the shadow of the Blackpool Tower, but he didn't see the donkeys with their dark red collars and shiny coats: he didn't see the Blackpool Pier stretched out on his right or the ice-cream van starting to pack up. All he saw was a pair of fine eyes and the sweetest smile. He'd lost count of the amount of times he'd had to pick Joshua up on the position of his hands. It was getting to the stage where he was doing it to annoy him, and it had worked. She hadn't been wearing a ring so, even if they were a couple they weren't official. But how someone as lovely as that chose to go out with a git like Joshua was beyond him. It wasn't any of his business, he told himself as he stood up and brushed the sand off his jeans. He was here to find those nuggets of gold for Lavender and then he was off fishing.

He found a little pizzeria not far from the guesthouse and, propping his book in front of him, glanced at it occasionally to put off any interruptions from the crowd of hen party revellers at the next table. God, he was too old for this game. He pretended to turn the page as he refused both coffee and pudding, instead just paying the bill there and then. He'd make his escape while they still let him: he'd already been asked to scrawl his name across the bride to be's ample bosom and now they were asking if he'd like to rate the bridesmaids out of ten. As he'd decided early on that none of them were worth more than a two (and that was him being generous) he made some excuse about meeting a friend and almost ran out of the restaurant.

Sitting on the steps staring out to sea, he finally decided it was time to give up dancing. He wouldn't let Lavender down but, after they'd whittled down the candidates to the last three pairs, he'd hang up his dancing shoes for good.

Apart from a couple of ambitious lovers, the beach was empty; empty and quiet. He could still make out the shadows on the sand from the twinkling lights cast from the South Pier; shadows only interrupted by the pools of water left by the falling tide. If he listened, he could just make out the sounds from the amusement arcade humming in the background but that was all. It was as if he was alone in the world, alone and…

He didn't know what made him turn except perhaps that new sense he seemed to have acquired earlier. He was being watched, and watched by her. How could that be? And yet, turning his head slightly, there she was standing on the steps down to the beach. He'd recognise her anywhere, even though she'd changed out of her bright pink leotard hours ago. He wouldn't deny he'd liked her in Lycra but she was prettier somehow, prettier and more vulnerable in a light summer dress sprinkled with flowers. Her hair, her wondrous hair had escaped the confines of her bun and now flowed across her shoulders and down her back almost reaching her waist. But it wasn't her dress or her hair he focused on. It was her face and the sheen of tears glistening in the gentle light.

Leaping to his feet he rushed to her side, dragging out a folded handkerchief from his pocket. 'Miss Markey, you're upset. How can I be of assistance?'

'It's nothing really. Don't worry about…'

'But I do, I am.' He thrust the handkerchief into her hand before taking her arm and leading her to one of the benches and helping her sit down.

'You're shivering,' he added, noting the tell-tale quivering on her skin with a frown. His eyes shifted to the rounded neckline and he clenched his jaw. It looked like she'd caught her dress with the way the top buttons had ripped through the fabric to be left hanging by a thread. She'd caught her dress or someone had tried to… He blinked. He didn't feel he knew her well enough to ask her about her relationship with

Joshua, but he hoped she'd tell him so he could help. After all she might very well have just caught the material on something… Any other cause was just too horrible to contemplate.

He shrugged out of his jacket and draped it across her shoulders.

'You're too kind.'

'I'm not being kind. I'm looking after our best dancer.'

She laughed, and he joined her in a smile. 'There, you see. It's not as bad as all that.'

Her laughter stopped. 'I'm afraid it is.'

'It is?'

'Joshua, *Mr Me I'm Called* Joshua has thrown me out.*'*

'Thrown you out?' He eyed her keenly, something lifting in his chest like a balloon suddenly filled with helium. 'I would have thought that would be something to celebrate. You can do better than him as a boyfriend.'

'That's the whole point.'

'I'm sorry, I don't quite understand?'

She'd picked up his hand and started playing with his fingers. He'd bet a pound she didn't even know what she was doing but whatever it was he never wanted her to stop.

'He's not my boyfriend. He's not really my dance partner. His wife's pregnant, as in heavily pregnant and once she couldn't fit into the costumes he'd ordered he went looking for a stand-in.'

He laughed, he couldn't help it. He'd never felt so relieved in his life at the thought of her not tangled up with that oaf. 'So, what's the problem? I think that's wonderful news.' He added, placing his hand around her shoulder but she pulled away and dropped his hand. He wished she hadn't.

'Really, it's all fine is it, Mr Hopper? It's all fine he's booked a double bed for the week and expects, *no,* demands I share it? He's taken both my bag and my suitcase so now I'm left with no alternative but to go back to him and, even if I manage to get my belongings there isn't a room to be had. I've just come from the Tourist Information Office and everywhere is booked solid.'

***

'A wedding ring?'

'Yes, er Beverley.' He grabbed her shoulders, pulling her to a stop outside the late-night jewellers presumably open late for just such an occasion as this. 'I hope you don't mind me calling you Beverley but as we're married it sort of goes with the territory. My name is Arnold.'

'I prefer Hopper.'

'So do I, as it happens but that's not really relevant. What is relevant is the fact that the owner of the guesthouse, lovely lady by the name of Susan Hall, thinks I am.'

'But why would she think that? You are married, aren't you?' Her eyes widened as all colour left her face. 'Oh God, out of the hands of one maniac and into the other.'

'No, and shush unless you want the whole of Blackpool in on our little secret,' he said, throwing a quick glance at the couple beside them.

'Darling,' he went on, his mouth now pressed into her neck. 'I always pretend I'm married, it's much gentler than telling them I'm not interested.' He felt her relax as she expelled her breath.

'Oh, oh I see. That's fine then, darling,' she replied, lifting her lips to his cheek.

It wasn't fine. It wasn't fine at all but it would have to do with the eyes of that couple still lingering. Taking her hand he opened the door and pushed her in first with a gentle hand. They'd get the ring and then he'd confront Joshua. He was looking forward to that part.

Breakfast was interesting as he examined Mrs Hall's raised eyebrows with a smile but as Beverley had a ring there was nothing she could do and it wasn't as if it was post-war or anything. Unmarried couples did live together. Okay, so they usually undressed in front of each other as opposed to hiding in the bathroom until the other one was in bed but he couldn't have everything. She'd nearly jumped out of her skin when he'd woken her by placing a cup of tea on her bedside table. He'd already showered and dressed but he didn't linger. She felt safe with him and that was something he wanted to continue. 'I'm just nipping out for the papers, anything you need?'

'No, I'm good. Hopper…' She grabbed his hand and gave it a little squeeze. 'Thank you for everything. Thank you for last night.'

'It was my pleasure,' he said with a grin, remembering the surprised look on Joshua's face when he'd barged in and demanded her bags. A threat to call the police not to mention his wife did the trick, especially as he hadn't been alone.

'I'll try and stay out of your way and not be a bother,' she added, releasing her hand to brush her hair off her forehead.

'You'll be no bother. I'll see you at breakfast.'

Lavender Peel called the group to attention with a clap of her hand.

'Right, as you may have heard Joshua Pratt has decided not to enter so, now we're a man short Hopper has kindly offered to step into his shoes so to speak. The next couple of days are make or break but now Guy is able to get around - albeit on crutches - he has also agreed to show his face. In effect, you have two experts to learn from, so learn.'

Hopper wasn't lucky. In fact you could say he was the unluckiest person around. He was the type of bloke to win a bottle of whiskey in the church raffle only to find he wasn't allowed to drink alcohol until he was eighteen. Apart from the whiskey, which he didn't really count as he'd only been six, the only thing he'd ever won was a deluxe hairdryer with all the accessories known to man, which was as useful to him as a pot of Brylcreem and a moustache trimmer. But weaving Beverley around the floor of the Rosebush Dance Studio he was the luckiest man in the world. She was as light as a feather on his arm and intuitively followed his steps and actions in perfect unison. He couldn't have felt closer if she'd been his twin but, with her sparkling blue eyes and the way her chestnut hair was coming adrift from her band to frame her face in a riot of curls, the one thing he didn't feel towards her was brotherly. Gentlemanly; yes. Brotherly; far from it. He never wanted the day to end because when it did, he'd have to relinquish his hold on this most perfect woman.

But end it did and, in the scuffle and scurry to leave the studio, he nearly lost her in the crowd of dancers heading down the road to the pub. Tomorrow was the day Lavender would decide on which three couples were going to enter the dance festival. Tomorrow he might be looking forward to a few more days in her arms. But the likelihood was he'd be rummaging around in the back of his Ford Escort for his fishing rod and tackle.

Standing at the bar while he waited to be served, he remembered with a smile that he still had the evening to look forward to. She was sharing his room, if not exactly his bed and, although not his wife, at least she was pretending to be.

'Who's having a vodka and lime,' he asked, placing the tray of drinks in the middle of the table before handing her a glass of dry white wine with a smile.

'Are you not drinking?' her gaze on his glass of orange squash.

'No. I'll probably head off after this one. I'm quite tired.' He rested his head back against the brown leatherette banquette before folding one leg over the other. 'I'm the old man of the group you know,' he added with a wink as he threw a glance across at Malcolm, Paddy and the other male members all posturing in their tightly fitting jeans as they made plans to hit the nightclubs later.

'Not that much older, surely?' Her voice soft as she leant towards him.

'Old enough, forty next birthday.'

'That's nothing. You're only a few years older than me.'

He raised his eyebrows.

'Thirty-two next birthday, which just happens to be next week so thirty-one and a half.'

'Shouldn't that be three-quarters or nine-eights?' he said, a mock frown wrinkling up his forehead.

She laughed. 'If I thought I could get away with saying thirty, or even better – twenty-nine, I would.' Bending down to pick up her bag she threw him a smile. 'I'm quite tired myself so I'll join you.'

'Surely you're not going already?' Margo said, throwing a quick glance across at Penelope. 'We're just going to get some grub and then find a dance floor.'

'What, you haven't had enough dancing for one day?' He grinned before taking Beverley's arm. 'We'll let you children enjoy yourself while we–'

'Go off somewhere quiet. We get it, don't we gang?' she added on a snort before turning away.

Hopper stared at the back of her sloppy peroxide dye job with a frown of annoyance and - it must be said - quite a bit of anger. He was all ready to walk over and confront her when he felt a tug on his arm.

'Don't let it bother you.'

'But they're insulting you?'

'I take it as a compliment. Come on, let's get some fish and chips and eat them on the beach.'

'Okay, but no skinny dipping, mind,' he said, shifting his arm to around her waist. 'I'm not sure if my blood pressure could stand it.'

'You can talk. What about that six-pack that was lurking under your t-shirt all afternoon?'

'More like a crate.'

***

'So, what do you do then, Hopper?'

'Have a guess.'

They were sitting on the beach, the chips a long distant memory, watching as the sun dipped into the sea. They'd found a quiet patch away from the night-time revellers but still within sight of the twinkly lights on the promenade and pier. The evening couldn't have been more perfect if she hadn't decided to sit as far away from him as possible. But, thinking about her most recent experience with the likes of Joshua, he couldn't really blame her.

She turned to look at him, taking her time to scroll up and down his body with a laugh. 'Oh, I don't know,' her eyes lingering on the area just above his belt. 'With a crate like that it has to be something like a bartender or nightclub owner?'

'Not a bad guess, but not even close. I'm a butler.'

'A butler.' Her eyes widened. 'You're having me on.'

She was bending over, tears dripping down her face in an explosion of laughter. 'You've been watching too much telly - that's your problem.' She glanced up at his silence and the laughter stopped as suddenly as it had started. 'OMG you're a butler. Well, I never. So what does the butler do again? Is he the one that opens the doors?'

'No, that would be Stevens, the footman.'

'Oh, he's the one that lays out his lordship's clothes and polishes his riding boots?'

'No. That would be Marsden the valet. I do get to have the keys of the cellar though,' he added with a smile.

'Well, at least that's something.'

'So what do you do, Beverley?' he said, rolling on his front and looking up at her.

'It's more a case of what I did.'

'I don't understand?' He took up a handful of sand before letting it run through his fingers and onto her arm.

'I'm a cook, or at least I was.'

'You were?'

'Yes. I was a cook at Joshua's restaurant but now obviously…' She looked up and pulled a face. 'But now, obviously I'm unemployed and probably sacked without a reference. With over eight million looking for work, it's unlikely I'll get a job.'

'Well, if you ever fancy going into service, and I wouldn't recommend it, the cook at the Cosgrave Manor has just handed in her notice.'

It was her breathing that alerted him first, her breathing and then the sound of muffled tears and then the scream.

In fact, if it hadn't been for the scream he'd probably have left her alone but there were other guests on the floor and the very last thing he wanted was a complaint going to Mrs Hall about the strange sounds coming from his bedroom. He was in a difficult position as it was with regards to his wife and, if she took it into her head to boot them out, they'd have nowhere to go.

Jumping out of bed he'd never been so thankful he'd packed his pyjamas. Not the most fashionable but, when he was being woken up constantly by his lordship, fashion didn't come into it.

'Shush it's alright,' he put his arm on her shoulder before brushing her hair off her forehead in the same way he did for Lady Sarah whenever she fell and scraped her knees. The screaming had stopped, thank God, but not the tears. Lifting her up into his arms, he positioned her head in the crook of his neck as he continued running his hand over her hair. 'It's alright Beverley, whatever you were dreaming about it's gone - long gone. It's only me and I'm never going to hurt you.'

'It was Joshua. I dreamt he… He tried to…'

'It's over, you're safe now.' He placed her back down on the pillows before tucking the duvet right up to her neck in an act of self-preservation before moving away to his side of the room.

'What about a cup of tea?' He said, looking down at his wrist. 'It's only three but I could do with a cuppa.' He watched as she scrambled out of bed, all his plans for her to be covered head to foot in the duvet disappearing in a puff of white nightie. 'Here let me. It's the very least I can do after interrupting your night's sleep.'

'I wasn't sleeping.'

She paused, kettle in hand.

'You weren't sleeping? What, you're one of them insomniacs or something?'

'No, I'm not used to sharing a room with…'

'A woman?'

'Anybody.'

Placing the kettle back on the table she walked over to him. 'I'm sorry, this must be really difficult for you.'

But she didn't continue. She couldn't continue. It was impossible for her to continue speaking with his lips clamped to hers in the sweetest of kisses – a kiss that went on and on and on…

'But I thought you weren't into women. I thought I'd be safe…' she said, confusion written all over her face as she grasped the neck of her nightie in a vice-like hand.

'I'm not into women, as such. I'm into one woman and she just so happens to be you.' He glanced away, his jaw tightening. 'But that doesn't mean you have to feel pressurised.' His gaze locking with hers again. 'That doesn't mean you have to feel anything other than safe.' He ran his hand through his hair before lifting his head. 'I have feelings for you, Beverley; strong feelings, the type of feelings that will never go away; the type that only grow stronger over time, never less. But also the type that never bind. Stay because you want to, or even if you don't want to. I'm happy to sleep on the beach if me staying here worries you,' he added, grabbing his bag and starting to stuff clothes in only to stop at the sound of her voice and then the soft feel of her fingers on his arm.

'I thought I was going mad, completely and utterly mad. I saw you and, as the song goes 'My heart went boom'. And then Joshua was so horrible and you came to my rescue like something out of a movie.' He watched a blush score up her cheeks. 'And then I thought I'd got it wrong, so wrong. You said you weren't into girls so I assumed that you were… well you know what I assumed, so I slammed the door shut on my feelings, my strong feelings.' She looked down at the ring on her finger; the ring they'd bought together before stroking her fingers along his arm and down to his hand.

'Beverley, I'm sort of old-fashioned, well I am a butler after all. I can't offer you much. I don't have much and, in a little over a week I'll be back at the beck and call of Lord and Lady Cosgrave.' He shook his head, trying to make sense of his thoughts. 'Come with me. We can spend whatever free time we have together and I'll even let you take over the care of the chickens,' he added, his eyes twinkling.

'Chickens. Well that makes all the other stuff immaterial now doesn't it? I'll come with you, Mr Hopper, but only because of the chickens,' she said, stepping closer. 'Now that we're a couple in the eyes of the world and married in the eyes of Mrs Hall do you think we can start our honeymoon?'

She didn't wait for a reply. In truth there wasn't a reply to be had. Instead, with both hands entwined through his hair she reached up and pressed her lips to his.

The End

Printed in Great Britain
by Amazon